Beyond the Veil

A Neverland Chronicles Novella

T.S. Kinley

First paperback edition November 2022
ISBN 979-8-9859074-4-5

Book design by T.S. Kinley
Editing by T.S. Kinley

www.TSKinleyBooks.com

AUTHOR'S NOTE

Beyond The Veil is a spicy romance novella. All characters in this book are above the age of eighteen. The content in this book contains sexually explicit depictions. Please be aware of the following possible trigger warnings and read at your own discretion. Lewd NSFW depictions of sexual acts, dubious consent, masturbation, drug use, violence, assault, hostage situations, and death.

Before you go. Follow T.S. Kinley on social media. Let's be friends! Check out our Instagram, Facebook, Pinterest, and Tic Tok pages and get insights into the beautifully, complicated mind of not one, but two authors! Have questions? Something you are dying to know about the amazing characters we've created? Join us online, we love to engage with our readers!

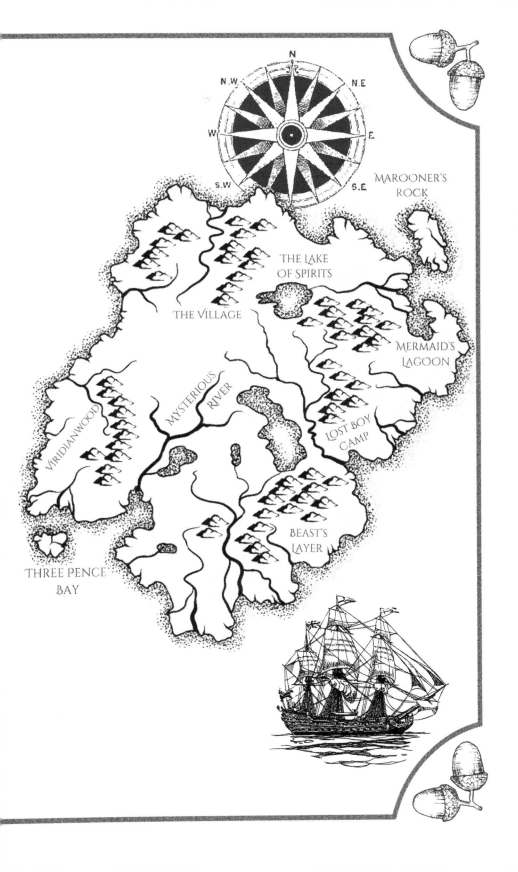

MAROONER'S
ROCK

THE LAKE
OF SPIRITS

THE VILLAGE

MERMAID'S
LAGOON

MYSTERIOUS RIVER

VIRIDIANWOOD

LOST BOY
CAMP

BEAST'S
LAYER

THREE PENCE
BAY

"The only way to get rid of a temptation is to yield to it. Resist it, and your soul grows sick with longing for the things it has forbidden to itself, with desire for what its monstrous laws have made monstrous and unlawful."
— Oscar Wilde, The Picture of Dorian Gray

Chapter One

DREAMS OF HER

PETER

I'd made the decision that I was going back across the Veil, no matter what they said. I was going for her, well I was going back for the next best thing, because she was gone. Gone like the boy I once was. Really and truly gone, in a place I could never bring her back from.

I awoke with my dick hard as a rock and groaned. I'd seen her again in my dreams, her beautiful face, sweet and pure, shining brightly in my minds eye. The dream had ended too soon, they always ended too soon, leaving me wanting, and in a foul mood. I'd dreamed of Wendy twice this week already. The dreams were increasing in frequency. I had kept my memories of Wendy mostly at bay, only thinking of her in particular circumstances. I preferred it that way. She had wreaked such havoc on my life, on my heart. I tried to avoid those emotions at all costs. But she had been my first, and to this day, my only love. That's not something you ever forget. I also couldn't forget how I hadn't been enough for her. She'd chosen to go back to our realm, for some chance at a life in that cruel world of unattained dreams. She had chosen *that* over me. She'd even used her silver tongue to lure my Lost Boys to go with her. I liked to pretend that it didn't bother me. That I'd been happy for them, but if I was being honest with myself, a small part of me had wanted to slit her throat for it.

I reached for the bowl sitting on my side table, fumbling for a familiar object. My hand rested on the cool textured metal of the thimble. Wendy's thimble. Her sweet 'kiss' was the only thing I had left of her. I rolled it in my fingers as my eyes explored all of its minute details. Holding it in my hand, I slid the other under the covers and began to stroke myself. I didn't take my eyes off the thimble the entire time. Starting off slow and measured, thinking of her as I pleasured myself. Remembering how her sweet, innocent features had morphed into that of a young woman. My rhythm picked up, becoming fevered, and sweat beaded on my brow as my mind entertained my darkest fantasies. My hand around her neck while I fucked her, my fingers leaving their marks on her pale skin, making her feel the physical pain that I'd felt when she'd left. With a groan, I reached climax. My hot seed covering my stomach in spurts. I laid there for a good while, reveling in my release before grabbing yesterday's shirt to clean up, feeling utterly dissatisfied.

I couldn't take this any longer. I needed more than just my own mental images. It was time to return across the Veil. Spring cleaning was just around the corner. I'd promised Wendy I would return every year to bring her back for spring cleaning, and that had extended to her daughters when she'd forgotten how to fly. I'd been avoiding going back across the Veil for the last few years. The Neverland Council had become more and more restrictive when it came to bringing humans back to Neverland. Irritatingly, my one vote on the Council had been overruled time and time again. They hadn't even allowed me to replace Gage after his unfortunate run-in with a certain pirate. I think they were hoping the absence would help me forget her, but it was only getting worse. The universe was tormenting me, telling me it was indeed time to go back, the Council be damned. I could no longer resist the urges, not with the dreams coming so frequently. I was being drawn there, and I didn't want to fight my fate anymore. It was time to bring the Lost Boys in on this. I would need their support if I was going to pull one over on the Council. I could always ask for forgiveness after she was already here, I was Peter fucking Pan wasn't I?

Chapter Two
LOST BOYS

I went to find Tripp first. He was my second in command, reliable to a fault. I could always count on him to have my back no matter the circumstances. He owed me, after all. I had gotten him out of that shit hole life he'd been living. He had been nothing more than skin and bones when I'd found him. I'm not sure if he realized how close he'd been to death at the time, but he never forgot what I'd done for him and he was incredibly loyal because of it.

Tripp had had the early morning watch so I trekked to the edge of camp and floated up to the crow's nest. I found him alert and scanning the landscape. He was always the most diligent with his responsibilities. Early morning watch wasn't all that bad, not when you got to see the beauty of Neverland in the gilded light of the rising sun. This morning, however, the skies were dawning overcast and a storm was looming just off the coast.

"What's got you up so early Pan? Dreams eatin' at ya again?" Tripp asked as he leaned against the rail of the crow's nest. His big form took up most of the available space. He was a few inches taller than I was, and his size almost rivaled that of the Neverland beasts.

"What gave me away?"

"Could be the foul mood radiating off of you, or could be the shit weather you've got brewing," he said as he motioned toward the darkening thunder clouds.

I grunted at this. It was never good to have your weaknesses so blatantly obvious. I'd never understood why or how Neverland was so sensitive to my mood. It irritated me that everyone on the island would know something was up with me today. Another reason that I needed to quell this Wendy obsession so I could move on with my life.

"I'm calling a meeting. I need all the Lost Boys present."

"OK, and what is it you need from me?"

"Who says I need anything from you?"

Tripp furrowed his brows and stared at me, waiting for me to get on with it.

"Alright, fine," I huffed. "I've decided to go back across the Veil and bring a daughter of Wendy back with me for this year's spring cleaning, and I need you to back me up on it."

The words came out in a rush. I knew that having him on my side would go along way toward convincing the others. Well at least Ryder anyway. Eben was an entirely different beast that I would deal with if it came to that.

His eyes went wide with surprise. I'd obviously caught him off guard, he hadn't been expecting this. He sighed before he answered. "I'm not going to ask what your intentions are with this girl you plan to bring back. I get it, you have some unresolved business with Wendy. If I go along with this, you have to promise me that you'll keep your shit together. That you won't make some innocent girl pay for Wendy's slights against you."

"Tripp, come on. How long have you known me? Have you ever seen me lose my shit?"

"I'm not going to answer that. But dealing with pirates is easy, dealing with girls that carry emotional baggage, is something altogether different. I wasn't here for the aftermath of Wendy, but if the stories are even remotely true, I don't want any part of that."

"I'm not about to ruin things here. I just want to enjoy the spring cleaning season, have a fucking fabulous May Day and then bring her back. I've not had a chance to celebrate May Day with a daughter of Wendy now that we get to fully participate in the festivities. It's just a few days and then she is gone, I promise." I tried to play it off like it was no big deal, like my insides weren't wrapped in knots while I waited to see if he would back me.

"Pan...don't make me regret this."

"I knew you'd have my back," I said haughtily and punched his shoulder. The thrill of excitement coursing through my veins. With Tripp backing me, it was as good as done. The girl would be mine, at least for a little while anyway. I just needed to go over the details with the others.

"Meet me in the old arms cellar. I don't want any nosy, gossiping faeries to figure out what I'm up to. The last thing I need is the Council getting wind of this."

Tripp nodded his agreement and I was off to rouse the other Lost Boys.

I went to see Ryder first. Putting pleasantries aside, I barged into his small house, too excited to wait. True to form, I was greeted with Ryder's bare ass while he pounded into some random Fae chick. She shrieked at the intrusion as she attempted to pull up the blankets to cover herself.

"What the fuck Pan, don't you knock anymore?" Ryder barked as he scrambled off the girl and covered his erection with a rumpled shirt. I smirked at him. With that handsome face, blonde hair and witty charm, that boy had half the population of Fae girls on this island lusting after him.

"Put your dick away and get dressed. There's a mandatory meeting at the arms cellar."

"Well can ya give me a minute to uh— finish things with Daphne here." He gestured to the petite brunette who was still staring at me wide eyed.

"*Now.* Your cock gets plenty of attention, I think you can

skip this one." I turned from the house then and slammed the door behind me to a flurry of curses from Ryder.

Now to find Eben. If anyone would give me trouble, it would be him. He was the most defiant of my Lost Boys. Always choosing to think for himself rather than just going along with my orders, that fucker. I probably would have gotten rid of him by now if he wasn't such a vicious fighter. Of all the Lost Boys, he was the most like me, and maybe that's what was so irritating about him.

I approached his house on the edge of camp with a bit more weariness. I took the time to knock, but I didn't wait for a response before letting myself in. Eben was sitting quietly in a chair, reading in the dim light from an oil lamp perched on the table. His dark features and all those tattoos covering his body gave him the look of a wraith in the darkness. He didn't even bother looking up from his book as I entered.

"What do you want Pan?" He said, completely deadpan.

I looked over at his bed before speaking and found Lilley-bell, still in her human form, curled up and sleeping under the covers. Her platinum blonde hair fanned out on the pillow.

"We need to talk," I said plainly, knowing he would get the gist that I wanted to talk alone.

"Lill," he called out to her and she stirred on the bed. "You gotta go. Get your shit and get out."

Lill sat up and rubbed the sleep from her eyes. I shook my

head. She was still trying in vain to get him to feel something for her, something other than just lust. She figured if she just kept throwing her body at him, the sex would somehow change his mind. It was insane thinking, but I guess I wasn't one to talk with my Wendy issues. She pouted as she collected her clothes, but said nothing at his curt dismissal.

"Peter," she said as she bobbed her head in acknowledgment before she morphed into her pixie form. A gust of air ruffled my hair and her tiny form flitted out the window.

"Do you really have to string her along like that? She is *my* faerie after all, you could treat her with a bit more respect," I scowled.

"Pan, you didn't come here to lecture me on my sex life, so get on with it, what do you need?"

"I need you in the arms cellar for a meeting. Now."

This got his attention and he looked up at me inquisitively. "What's going on?"

"Like I said, I need you all in the arms cellar. I'll give you the run down there. The others are already waiting."

Eben got to his feet in a huff, pulled on a shirt and some boots before he made to follow me.

Chapter Three
THE MEETING

I slid down the hatch in the tree stump and landed in the shadowed recesses of the subterranean arms cellar. The place that had once been my home with Wendy. I hadn't been able to live there after Wendy left. It sparked too many memories of the family I'd lost. But, it was one of the most secure locations in Neverland, and it offered a place where we could meet without the faeries looking over our shoulders.

"Alright, out with it Pan, what's got your balls in such a pinch that you had to drag me out of my house at dawn?" Eben asked.

I waited with an exaggerated pause, drawing out the

suspense just a little, to make sure they were all paying attention.

"I'm going back across the Veil," I stated. I purposefully left out the detail about the daughter of Wendy, for now at least.

"What, like for good?" Ryder asked, his brows drawn in confusion.

"No, definitely not. I just felt like it was time to revisit our old stomping grounds and—"

"You're going back for another girl, aren't you?" Eben interrupted, sparing me from the rambling explanation I was about to give. Well I guess we were getting right to the point, no use in avoiding it now.

"It's a possibility. If there is a Darling girl that's of age and willing to come back with me."

"Jesus Christ Pan, you're a damned glutton for punishment. You think you'd have learned your lesson the first time. What's the benefit of bringing a human girl back here? There is none."

"Now look," I snapped, my irritation growing with his insubordination. "I made a promise to Wendy that I would return for spring cleaning every year, and that extends to her daughters as well. I've held off for many years on account of the Council's whims, but it's time for me to make good on my promise and at least offer her the opportunity."

"So you want us to go along with a ridiculous promise you made to a girl when you were thirteen years old? That was over a hundred years ago in Earth's time. Wendy is long dead and the idea of Peter Pan is nothing more than fantasy to her descendants."

My mood darkened at his comments. His words touched on some of my worst fears. That Peter Pan was nothing more than a myth to Wendy's daughters.

"You don't know that for certain. You of all people believed the stories, you believed them so much that you sought me out. I'm still waiting for the story on how you figured out how to get across the Veil on your own." I reminded him. One way to shut Eben up was to start asking questions about his past. "And even if they did forget, maybe it's time I reminded them that Peter Pan does exist."

"And when the girl leaves, what then? Are you going to self destruct, like you did when Wendy left? It seems like a weak move, why bring back the one thing that can bring you to your knees? It's like you want to serve Neverland up on a platter to Captain Hook."

"Really Eben, learn to have a little fucking fun. I'm going to bring the girl back to Neverland, enjoy the May Day festivities and then bring her back. Aren't you tired of looking at the same Fae girls? Wouldn't it be nice to have a human girl here? Change things up a bit."

"I think it's a bad idea Pan. You're playing with fire and we're the ones that will have to pay the price when Neverland exacts her punishments for your behavior."

"What say you, Ryder?" I asked, ignoring Eben

completely. He'd been unusually quiet as I'd had a war of words with Eben.

He looked visibly uncomfortable at being pulled in between our spat and took his time answering. "I trust you Pan. If you say it'll just be an extra girl to celebrate May Day with, then I'm good with that. Just as long as you're okay with me knocking some sense into ya if you start acting crazy over this girl."

"See, both Ryder and Tripp think it'll be fine."

Eben scowled and clinched his hands into fists. "Fine! Do whatever you want, just know that I was against this when the whole thing falls to shit."

"Well lucky you, you're not the one that gets to make the decisions, but I'll take your coerced approval anyway. I know I don't need to say this, but everyone needs to keep their mouths shut about this. I don't want the Council sabotaging my plans. They have sentries placed all throughout the realm. I want to keep them in the dark on this or else they will make getting across the Veil fucking hell. Ryder, I'm looking at you."

"What? Like I can't keep this shit to myself," Ryder exclaimed.

"Your mouth has a tendency to get loose whenever someone's stroking your cock," Tripp chided. They were the first words he'd spoken since the meeting began, allowing me to work things out with Eben without ganging up on him. He really was a better man than I'd ever be.

"Now that everything's settled, I'm going to start making a few trips across the Veil just to check things out before I bring her back with me. I'll need you all to run cover for me with the rest of the Fae."

"Are you going to tell Lill?" Eben asked.

I scowled at this, Lill would definitely not approve of me bringing back a daughter of Wendy. I would have to think about what I would do with the overprotective and insanely jealous pixie before I brought a girl back with me. "Let me handle Lill. Just...don't say anything to her now. Got it?"

Everyone nodded. I wrapped my knuckles twice on the center table, signaling to the others that the meeting was concluded.

Chapter Four
CHECK AND MATE

I slumped into my bed at dawn after the long trip from beyond the Veil. It had been more tedious than I'd expected. I'd had to evade Fae sentries along the way. There were more than I had remembered. I'd agreed to posting them when it had been recommended by the Council, but there were a lot more than I'd been led to believe. It was something I would need to address at the next Council meeting. There was no need to waste such man power guarding the Veil.

My thoughts drifted then, to the young woman I'd found at the Darling home. I'd first seen her, sound asleep in her bed. A cascade of chestnut brown hair curled around her pale face. Her expression peaceful in the depths of sleep. If I'd had any doubts about bringing her back with me, they'd gone out the window the moment I saw her. I knew I'd return to her every night until it was time to bring her back. I already couldn't wait to see her again, to watch her and see what she was like and how she compared to Wendy.

I was completely lost in thought when Lilleybell flitted through my window, faerie dust trailing in her wake. I rolled my eyes, I was exhausted and I wasn't prepared to deal with her now. She landed on my chest and placed her hands on her hips, demanding my attention.

"What do you want Lill?" I said as I glared down at her.

"Where were you last night?" She questioned, her words nothing more than a soft tinkle of bells.

"I had a thing I had to see to," I responded vaguely.

"Don't play coy with me, Peter Pan. I know you're up to something. Even the boys are acting out of sorts. Eben's been ignoring me since you came to see him."

I sighed, trying to think of any way I could avoid this interrogation without giving away my mission. As much as I hated it, I was going to have to lie to her. I'd been mulling it over in my head, trying to figure out a way that I could get rid of her during spring cleaning without hurting her feelings. She could be a full-on thorn in my side when she got emotional.

"Okay Lill, I'll be straight with you." I stalled as an idea formed in my head. I had to think on the fly and make my case as believable as possible. So I decided to let her in on some half truths and embellish the shit out of them. "We've come across some very valuable information. Stories have been coming in that a five masted clipper has been spotted sailing in the In Between, and there are rumors it's Blackbeard himself."

Her eyes went wide at the notion, "Seriously?"

"Uh-huh, and did you know that once upon a time, our very own Captain Hook was his bo'sun. Blackbeard is the stuff of legends. The last thing we need is another band of pirates in Neverland. It would throw the balance of power in their favor. I have to watch the situation closely."

"What are you going to do?"

This was the question I'd been waiting for, time to work my magic and seal the deal by playing off of her heart strings.

"I was planning on sending Eben on a recon mission. He's my best fighter. It will take someone with his skill set to have any chance at survival if something goes wrong. I hate to send him, but I need someone to hunt down this ship. Find out who the captain is, what their plans are, and report back to me."

"You would send him out there with no back up?" Her little cheeks began to flush as her anger brewed under the surface.

"I can't spare any more men. It's almost May Day so the Fae won't send any of their fighters. It's my job to stay one step ahead of the pirates. I have to send someone. If only I had someone who could slip in undetected and with the extra speed to get away. Eben's a bigger target and slower than the Fae, but my hands are tied on this."

"What about me? I could go? I'm small and fast. No one would even know I was there and I could get back here much quicker than Eben ever could." She sounded desperate as she pleaded.

Check and mate. I had her exactly where I wanted her. A mission like that could take her weeks to accomplish. I'd have hell to pay when she realized no such ship sailed the In Between, but I'd have time to come up with a suitable excuse.

"You know, you were my first choice. Your recon skills are much better than Eben's, but I didn't want to ruin your May Day."

"It's fine, it's no big deal. There's always next year. Plus, I wouldn't enjoy May Day if I was worrying the whole time about Eben," she said dejectedly. I hated tricking her into this farce of a mission, but now that she'd given her word, the deal was set.

"Thank you Lill for volunteering. Eben doesn't deserve your affections. You know there are others that would have helped you enjoy May Day," I said, trying to offer her some comfort for her unrequited affections. Lill and I were friends with the occasional benefits. And even though it didn't go beyond friendship, I still cared about her.

"Thanks, Peter." She smiled softly and placed a tiny kiss on my chin. "I'm going to start getting things prepared for my trip. I'll plan to leave the day after tomorrow," she said, looking for my approval.

"Sounds good Lill. When you get back, I promise I'll make it worth your while." She turned to go, but I called out to her, "and Lill... just keep this mission from the other Fae. I don't want to cause any panic until I know what we're dealing with." She nodded her agreement and flitted out the window. I breathed a deep sigh of relief now that Lill was taken care of. As soon as she was gone, I'd make my final trip across the Veil and bring back the daughter of Wendy. The day after tomorrow couldn't get here fast enough.

Chapter Five
DAUGHTER OF WENDY

The next morning, I had breakfast with the boys. I decided to tell them about this new daughter of Wendy, and how I'd gone back across the Veil last night to observe her. I'd watched as she laid, lazily in her bed, reading a book. I'd been entranced by her, even this mundane activity had captured my full attention. Her long, elegant fingers turning the pages, the crease in her brow as she absorbed the story, the occasional little laughs that would catch me off guard. I'd finally pulled myself from her window when she'd drifted off to sleep with the book draped over her breasts.

"Do you think she'll agree to come back with you?" Tripp

asked. I hadn't even thought about asking her. I'd decided she was coming with me, her choice in the matter hadn't been relevant.

"I'm Peter Pan, she's a daughter of Wendy, that's just how it works. There won't be any problems, she'll agree to come back with me," I said with absolute conviction.

"What does she look like? Is she hot?" Ryder asked. Damn he could be so shallow sometimes.

"Seriously Ryder, does it matter?"

"Well, no but—"

Ryder was interrupted when a rustle arose from the forest beyond the camp. All of us raised from our seats in one fluid motion, instantly on high alert. Within moments a detail of satyrs and nymphs entered the clearing. These weren't just any fighters. They were armed to the teeth, their leather armor embossed with the seal of the Princess. This was Tiger Lily's personal guard. What were they doing at my camp? I knew this wasn't good. They never showed up uninvited or unannounced. I glanced around at the boys. It was clear that they were thinking the same thing. It wasn't a coincidence that Tiger Lily's guard showed up after I'd started plotting to bring a daughter of Wendy back to Neverland.

"Silas," I said as I strode over to the Captain of the guard and greeted him formally. "What brings you to my camp this fine morning?" My tone was clipped and it was clear that I wasn't pleased with their unexpected visit.

"Pan, forgive the intrusion, but Tiger Lily is requesting an audience with you."

"Is that so? And she sent her lackeys to come collect me?"

He didn't respond, just shuffled his feet. I could tell that he didn't enjoy carrying out the task he'd been assigned, not when it meant collecting the notorious Peter Pan for his Princess.

"Well you can remind Tiger Lily that I am Peter Pan, and I cannot be summoned like a dog. I will be finishing my breakfast. When I have time to fit her into my day, I'll grace her with my presence," I stated firmly. Making it obvious that I wouldn't stand for any arguments on this. He nodded his agreement and the entire band of guards receded into the forest, leaving us alone in the clearing.

"Who opened their mouth?" I seethed.

"It wasn't me, I swear, I've not said a single thing to anyone!" Ryder said in a whoosh. I stared at him a moment, and the genuine look of shock on his face told me it hadn't been him.

"Come on Pan, you know none of us would say anything." Eben leered at me.

"Well why is Tiger Lily's guard at my doorstep? I get the feeling it's not because she's missed my company. She knows something and I'm going to figure out which one of you has a loose tongue."

"Pan, we've kept things pretty tight since you laid out

your plan. I don't think any of us are the rat you're looking for," Tripp said matter-of-factly.

"Exactly and I expect you to grovel at our feet when you realize that you're wrong. We may be a lot of things Pan, but we're not snitches and we're all loyal to this group." Eben turned then and stalked off, his hands fisted at his sides.

Chapter Six

TIGER LILY

I hung around the camp for a while after breakfast. I'd planned to get a little sleep after my trip last night. But my hackles were up after our visitors this morning. I couldn't go running to Tiger Lily, I wasn't some subordinate that she could order around at her leisure. I had to leave her waiting, to stew over the fact that I'd not come running when she'd called. I'd paced the central clearing, running scenarios through my mind, considering all the angles and every excuse I could use. My mind was going a mile a minute. Tripp, having noticed my erratic behavior had insisted we spar in the ring, allowing me to work off some steam as we traded punches. It was exactly what I needed.

IT WAS TIME. I headed to the village. I'd put it off as long as I could. Sparring with Tripp had settled my nerves and I felt prepared to handle whatever urgent need Tiger Lily wanted to talk about. I centered my mind as I walked through the small village. Tiger Lily's guards wasted no time ushering me into her home. They were obviously expecting me. The dwelling was awash in natural light as the sun filtered in from the skylights above. The interior of her home was comfortable and meticulously clean. Large cushions were positioned in the center of the room around a tawny fur that was laid out like a rug. Everything was decorated in vibrant colors, natural woods and gold tones. Tiger Lily sat at the table in the corner pouring out two cups of tea, not even bothering to look up at me. She was clothed in a white woven tunic dress, trimmed with the cream colored tails of some small animal and cinched together with a braided leather belt. The dress complimented her warm, caramel skin. She was the most beautiful nymph on the island. She was keenly aware of it too. She was skilled at using it as a weapon in her arsenal.

"Peter, my friend, sit down and have some tea with me.

It's been too long since we've had the chance to talk." Her voice was sugary sweet and it put me more on guard. I walked over and took a seat next to her.

"Why do I get the feeling this is more than just a social call."

She tsked in disapproval, "Oh Peter, you're too perceptive for your own good."

"Well as much as I enjoy your company, I'd rather skip the evasive shit and get to the point. What do you want from me?"

"What I want from you is answers."

"Feel free to ask whatever question you want, and then I'll decide if I'll give you an answer."

She lifted her gaze from her tea cup and stared at me, her dark eyes were cold and calculating, a far cry from her soft and sultry voice. Those eyes didn't miss a thing. I got the distinct feeling that I was in the presence of a predator. She had to be. It was the only way she kept reign over all the Fae in Neverland.

"You and I are old friends, maybe even more than just friends," she insinuated. She slid her hand across the table to run her fingers suggestively over my forearm. The movement was meant to be seductive, and yet it only put me on edge. I simply cocked my head in response, not fully agreeing with her statement. "With that in mind, I won't let you wriggle like a worm on a hook." She paused then and took a long sip of her tea, drawing out the moment. "I'm going to tell you a little story. I received a visit from our mutual friend, the pixie Lilleybell."

Fuck— it had been Lill that had snitched on me to Tiger Lily. But if that was true, then she didn't know the whole story. However, Tiger Lily would be much harder to fool than Lill. She continued to lay out her story and I knew I had to keep quiet, lest she catch me in a lie.

"She'd come to tell me that she would be unavailable to assist with this year's May Day celebration. I thought to myself, how odd. Lilleybell had always been an eager partici-pant. When I questioned her, she hesitated, then she provided me with an obvious lie. My own subject, lying to her Princess. I know there is only one person that she would ever lie for— and that's you." She stopped then and waited. I wasn't sure what she wanted me to say and my brain was screaming at me to deny the whole thing.

"I don't know what you want me to say. It sounds like your problem is with Lill."

"Peter, you underestimate me if you think Lilleybell didn't tell me every little detail about the 'mission' you planned to send her on."

"And so, what's your point? We all needed a break from Lill. She's formed an unhealthy attachment to Eben and I wanted to make sure he had a good time this May Day. So I sent her on a harmless mission. She'll be none the wiser and we'll ensure that May Day is drama free." I tried to play it off like it was no big deal, as much as it pained me to rest all of the blame on Lilleybell's shoulders.

She clicked her tongue at me and smiled deviously, as if I'd walked right into her trap.

"Peter did I not just tell you not to underestimate me? I know that you've been sneaking across the Veil. Not just once, but two nights in a row. And if you think that I did not place some of my best spies to watch over the Darling home, then you truly are naive."

There it was, she knew everything. I'd been duped, deceived and out witted. She was right, I had been naive, naive in thinking that the Council hadn't taken a vested interest in the Darling family. Wendy or not, the Darling family and the descendants of all the previous Lost Boys were a liability for Neverland. How could I have been so stupid as to think they would forget. I swallowed hard, my mind racing, trying to figure out what I could say to salvage this. I wouldn't give up this daughter of Wendy so easily. My ranking matched that of Tiger Lily's here in Neverland. I needed to meet her head on.

"Alright, and what is your plan now that you've discovered my little secret?"

"You do realize that this little tryst of yours could endanger the whole of Neverland. Are you really that selfish?"

"It won't happen like it did with Wendy, I won't allow it. I've brought them back with me before and managed to dutifully return them back across the Veil without incident. This time will be no different."

"I know you've been dreaming of her. I've been dreaming of her too. I believe we are at a crossroads here and we need to choose our steps carefully."

"How did you know that I'd been dream—"

"That is not a productive question we need to focus on right now. I have a bargain for you. If you agree to my terms and fulfill the bargain, then I will keep this information to myself and not alert the rest of the Council to your plans."

"And how do I know that the other sentries won't pass this along to the rest of the Council? If any of them went digging, wouldn't they come across the same information that you did?"

"The sentries are Fae and I am their Princess. I have given the order that they are to speak to no one about this but me, but I have only to give the word, and they would send a convoy to update the entire Council on what you've been up to."

She had me by the balls. Either agree to her bargain or be ousted, and see my plans for the daughter of Wendy destroyed. I'd likely lose my seat on the Council.

"What is it that you want?"

"You must agree first and then I will tell you what I want from you."

"Fine, just get on with it."

"There is an old artifact that I am looking to acquire, a magical relic of sorts. I need you to retrieve it for me."

"What sort of relic? And where do I find it."

"It's a bone, a skull from a very powerful creature. It comes from the first realm and it is the prized possession of the bone faerie."

My eyes went wide as I thought of the old hag that lived in the deep recesses of the Viridianwood. A place where no other man, beast or Fae ever ventured.

"You're joking right? You want me to steal a magical skull from the old bone hag? That's like taking candy from a babe. She probably couldn't even see me coming if I walked straight in through her front door. Navigating the Viridian-wood might be a bit tricky, but nothing the Lost Boys and I can't handle."

She laughed quietly for a moment, "Peter, I sometimes question how it is that you've lived this long. Appearances aren't always what they seem. The bone faerie isn't native to Neverland. She is a transplant, like you. She is from the 1st realm, and she is ancient. She's been in hiding here for reasons unknown. Something altogether more wicked than either of us can fathom, has chased her here. She has kept herself hidden, but don't let that fool you into thinking that she isn't lethal. Lethal in ways that you couldn't begin to understand, and that makes you a vulnerable target."

"Why haven't you collected this item yourself? You could

have sent your highly trained armed guards in to fetch it for you. Why me? Why now?"

"I have my reasons... but I will give you as much information as I can, so you will be prepared."

"What's so important about this relic anyway? Why do you want it so badly that you're willing to blackmail me just to get your hands on it."

"It's important to the balance of power in Neverland. It will help to tip the scales in our favor. There's unrest in the realms and we've been playing host to more and more refugees. Neverland has always been a dumping ground for those running from their own worlds. It's only a matter of time before someone with malicious intent invades our shores. Consider it my secret weapon."

"I guess, if that's what it takes to buy your silence. But I need to know everything you know about this... bone faerie."

"Of course. I wouldn't think of sending you in there blind. But first, let us celebrate this little agreement we've come to, shall we?" Her demeanor shifted once the deal had been brokered. She smiled at me coquettishly, "How's the tea?" She asked, her tone dripping with innocence.

I stared down at my half empty cup and took inventory of my body, my mind whirling at what she could have spiked my tea with. I felt instantly flushed and my heart rate began to quicken.

"What did you put in my tea?" I asked as I pushed back

from the table. It wasn't altogether unpleasant and my cock stirred of its own accord.

"Oh just a little aphrodisiac recipe I concocted. It should be reaching full effect any moment now," she said seductively. She stood from her chair and walked over to me, lifting her dress and straddling me. The feel of her body sent a rush of pleasure through me as she brushed against my cock, that was now hard as nails, thanks to the tea.

"Isn't that nice," she purred as she ground her hips against my erection.

"Damn it Tiger Lily, I'm not in the habit of having sex with women who've just fucked me over."

"See I knew you would be no fun after our chat. That's why I helped you along with the tea. I didn't want you to be in a foul mood when you left. I wanted us to seal the deal with a truly carnal act. Trust me, you'll feel better afterwards." She continued to grind on me while her lips found my neck, curling her fingers in my hair.

"You want me to trust you? I think that's the last thing I should be doing right now. I wouldn't put it past you to slit my throat once I make you cum." I tried in vain to think of something, anything other than fucking her, but I couldn't push my mind past the desperate need pulsing in my cock.

She laughed at my comment, "Well then it's a good thing I like you Peter." She bit down hard on my shoulder and sent a shudder of pain and pleasure coursing through me. I was done with talking now. There was no scenario in which I left this house before I finished what she'd started. I grabbed her ass and stood up suddenly. She let out a low growl, obviously pleased with herself. I walked to the large bed that was situated across the room and threw her down. She'd tricked me into this, therefore I had no incentive, no obligation to make it good for her.

"Turn over," I commanded.

She bit her lip and stared up at me for a moment before she complied. I knew better than to think she was being obedient. She wanted it like this. I pushed up her skirt to expose her round, perfect ass. I took in the sight of her as I unbelted my pants, my cock springing free of its constraints.

Her pink cunt was glistening with her arousal and my cock twitched, eager to be inside of her. The cool air on my heated skin sent a shiver through me. I grabbed myself at the root with one hand and grasped her hip, tight in the other. I entered into her warm folds with a hiss, and she matched me with a gentle moan. I stayed there a moment, fully sheathed inside her. She began to shake her hips, encouraging me to give her the friction she so desperately wanted. I reached up and wrapped her long, ebony hair around my palm and pulled her head back.

"This is what you wanted? You wanted me to fuck you like this?"

She stayed silent, only her heavy breathing filled the room. I began to pull out of her slowly, leaving just the tip inside her.

"Say it, or I'll leave you just like this and finish myself off."

"Yes," she whispered.

"What was that? I didn't hear you."

"Yes!" She demanded, and I slammed into her.

She cried out, but I kept going. The need inside me unleashing my primal nature. Pounding into her at a frenzied pace, I focused on my own pleasure. Images of the girl from beyond the Veil clouded my mind. I stared at the ceiling, concentrating on only her. I may have been in the room, fucking Tiger Lily, but my mind was ravaging my mystery girl. I could feel my balls tighten and I allowed myself to slip over the edge. I pulled out of her and blew my load all over her perfect ass. I stood over her for a moment, letting my mind clear and then I tucked myself back into my pants and turned to leave.

"Hey, what the fuck, Peter?' Tiger Lily called from behind me. I ignored her and kept walking toward the door. "Get back over here and finish what you started... Peter... Peter!"

I slammed the door behind me without even looking back. Tit for tat, if she was going to play games with me, I would throw it right back at her. I smiled to myself as I headed home, smug in the knowledge that I'd won that round.

Chapter Seven

ARE YOU REALLY THAT SELFISH

We flew over the Viridianwood, covering as much distance as possible in the air. With the limited information I'd been given from Tiger Lily and a few trusted Fae sources, we had decided that the general location of the bone faerie's home should be at the heart of the forest. It was one of the only locations in Neverland where I had not yet ventured.

We landed, silently on the moss covered ground with massive trees towering over our heads. The canopy above was so thick, that the landscape below appeared to be in perpetual twilight. We fanned out to cover more ground, but kept in sight of each other. It would be a mistake to split up here. We moved through the thick underbrush slowly, each of us with a weapon poised in hand. Scanning the surroundings for potential threats. The handle of my dagger dug into my palm as I gripped it tighter than I needed to.

This forest was alive, and it felt as though it was watching our every move. A symphony of sounds filled the air around us, leaves crunching underfoot, unknown creatures scurried at the arrival of intruders in their midst. The delicate swish of the branches as they brushed past our bodies, grabbing at our clothes, like skeletal hands. Strange, blue orbs were fading in and out of view. Something unseen, rustled in the dead leaves at my feet. I paused silently, the sound disappearing as quickly as it came. A pair of glowing, orange eyes, stared out at me from a hollowed out tree.

"This place gives me the fuckin' creeps," Ryder complained. "I'll take pirates any day over this shit."

"You owe us big time after this, Pan. It was one thing going along with your ridiculous plan for this Wendy girl and now you've roped us into this shit. If I die, I'm taking you with me," Eben said. It was always fucking sunshine and roses with him.

I rolled my eyes. I'd just come to terms with the fact that we were going to be at odds until I brought the girl back home after May Day.

"Just shut up and keep your eyes open. I don't want to be here when it gets dark. We need to get this done today."

I heard a familiar whistle and turned in the direction of

the call. I could see Tripp between the trees ahead of us. He was crouched on the ground, examining something. I came through the brush to find a circular patch of land that was devoid of any life. The ground was black and littered with bones. Drab scraps of thread-bear clothing still clinging to some of them. Swords, their metal still polished and shining, lay useless beside the piles of remains.

"Looks like a band of pirates met their maker here," Tripp explained as he held up a rumpled tricorn hat. "I'm wondering if this is the work of your bone faerie. Some of the bones are missing. I'm counting eleven bodies, I think, but I can't be sure since the skeletons aren't in tact. The skulls are all gone and the femur bones seem to be missing too."

I scanned the area for clues to what might have happened. It looked as though they were simply marching through the woods. There wasn't any obvious sign of a struggle or fight. How could one old faerie take out a small band of pirates? These men were no strangers to fighting for survival and it looked like they hadn't even had a chance.

"No wonder Tiger Lily didn't send her own men after her latest obsession, she knew it was a death trap. You shouldn't have messed with her Pan. I'm starting to think she wants you dead," Ryder said. His comments didn't seem too far off the mark either. Maybe she did want me dead. I was probably an affront to her. She'd been born to rule Neverland, while I'd had to acquire my role here. The island was itself a living, sentient being of sorts, that could pick and choose who it bestowed and denied power to. Maybe Tiger Lily could never get over the fact that Neverland had chosen me.

"Collect the weapons and anything else of value. Take a few of the bones as well. Maybe we can use them as offerings," I barked out my command. I needed everyone to focus on the task at hand before their imaginations got the better of them. To be brave, an element of fear was necessary, but too much could render a fighter completely useless.

We continued on, seemingly on the right path if the dead pirates were any indication. It wasn't long before I caught a glimpse of movement in my peripherals. I halted my forward progress and signaled to the others who quickly picked up on the movement as well. Whatever it was, it didn't seem to be coming towards us. We all took up positions, flanking the creature as we moved in to try to get a better look.

As we got closer, I realized it was a man, a pirate. His hunched form shuffled through the woods, swaying as if he was drunk. He stared blankly ahead, stumbling along as he mumbled incoherent words. I positioned myself in front of him and stepped from the shadows directly into his path. It was a gamble for sure, but his current condition didn't give off the impression that he was any kind of a threat.

"How goes it pirate?" I asked. My voice sounding foreign in this odd place. The man stopped abruptly and looked up at me with wide eyes. His face was gaunt and crusted with grime. His ragged clothes hanging from his body. The deep V neck of his shirt revealed part of his sunken torso, each rib, painfully prominent. The man was emaciated and unkempt. He'd obviously been wandering the forest for a long time. He dropped to his knees in front of me.

"Please, good spirit, end my suffering," he pleaded in a hoarse voice that was nearly unintelligible.

"I can end your suffering, but you must tell me how you came to be here first."

"She torments me as I wallow. I've kept them to myself and she is none pleased." He chuckled dryly and then fell into a fit of coughing.

"Who torments you? The bone faerie?" I demanded, grabbing his bony shoulders and pulling him up to face me.

"We shouldn't be here, it's madness. Her vengeance doesn't abide by the rules."

"Tell me what you know? How does she fight? Did she kill your comrades?" I continued to press him even though his answers made little sense.

"You can't see what's coming and I can't withstand the draw any longer. But the magic does not dwell here... she will be so disappointed and I will revel in it." He smirked and then spit on the ground. "Let it be over. Let her find that she is wrong. I am no one, nobody. This life will give her nothing... NOTHING! You hear me... nothing!" He screamed in my face and used his last vestiges of energy to push me away from him, breaking my grasp on his shoulders. He drew his sword, barely able to pull it from its scabbard, and charged at me. It was a decrepit attempt to engage me in battle.

Nothing more than a desperate act to illicit a response, force my hand into a fight he did not intend to win. He ran himself through on my dagger, his eyes growing wide as my blade pierced under his ribcage and up into his chest cavity.He let out a whoosh of breath, ladened with blood that splattered on my face. His listless body began to sink and I followed him toward the ground, my dagger still stuck in his chest.

"Finally. Thank you." His final words came out in a wheezy breath and his limp body fell, on the ground as I yanked my dagger free of his body.

"What the fuck was that?" Ryder exclaimed.

"Just the ramblings of a dead man walking. Who knows how long he's been wandering around the forest alone. Between that and the lack of food, his mind's gone soft," I reassured him.

The odds of completing this task for Tiger Lily seemed to be getting more and more grim. These men had simply wandered into the wrong part of the forest. They hadn't been attempting to steal the bone faeries most prized possession and still they had met a dreadful end.

"Keep moving," I commanded and began to head deeper into the woods.

"Hang on," Eben called to me. I whirled on him, ready to have it out with him if he planned to challenge me on completing this mission. He was pulling a hatchet from his belt as he eyed the body on the ground.

"We should take the head. She left most of the other

bones, but she took every skull. Seems like she has a preference."

He swung his hatchet in a powerful arc, separating the head from the body in one swing. Grabbing a handful of hair, he picked up the head, wrapping it in the shirt he stripped from the pirates body. Securing it to his belt, he nodded at me to proceed, his face splattered with blood.

"WHAT THE F—" I sighed raking my hands through my hair in desperation. It was the third time we'd come across the pirate's body— we were walking in circles. No matter which way we'd gone, we'd ended up returning to the same spot. It was infuriating.

"Maybe we should head back to camp and regroup, figure out a better plan because this just isn't working," Ryder stated. He'd been biding his time all day waiting for the perfect opportunity to offer up some feasible excuse to retreat. He was a fierce fighter, but not much of a fan when it came to magic.

"This isn't over. The missions not lost yet. If we just—" My train of thought was distracted as the glow of a pixie flitted into our midsts.

"Lill? What are you doing here?" I asked, shocked to see

her. I scowled a bit, she was the last person I wanted to see. She knew that I'd tried to send her on a sham mission and I hadn't figured out how I was going to explain myself. I wasn't big on apologies.

"I knew you'd never find the bone faerie without Fae help. So I took pity on you guys and decided to offer up my talents." Her chimed response was smug.

"We would've found her on our own, but since you're here and I'm pressed for time, I'll accept your offer to help."

"Hmm, sure you could have. Was walking in circles part of your great plan?" She smirked.

"Just get on with it Lill."

"Well anyone who is trying to track down a powerful Fae, can't just wander around the woods aimlessly. She uses that magic to hide her location. You didn't even realize that she is sending you in circles. I thought you were smarter than this Peter?" She chuckled as she explained, delighting in the fact that she knew more than me on this subject.

"I fight pirates, not faeries. I've never had to track down a Fae before." My excuse sounded weak.

"Magic leaves a residue behind. It's almost impossible to detect, except for those with a highly trained eye and lucky for you, I'm just such a pixie."

"You're telling me you can see magic residue?"

"It's just one of my many talents, right Eben?"

Eben grumbled at the insinuation.

"Well then, what are you waiting for? Quit your boasting and make yourself useful already."

Lill pursed her petite lips in irritation but set about her task without further comment. The four of us followed behind her in silence, all of us ready to get this over with and get home.

True to her word, Lill guided us to a section of the woods that I hadn't seen before and I couldn't comprehend how we'd missed it altogether. She paused as we reached a massive boulder.

"Her home is through there," she pointed to a crack in the stone that appeared just wide enough for a man to fit through.

"Alright, we'll walk around, it shouldn't take us long," I said.

"You can try and go around, but you will never find her house on the other side. You must go *through* the crack to get there," She insisted.

"Going through the crack isn't a good idea. She could easily pick us off one by one if we go in there," I countered, hoping she could give me some other option.

"If you want to see the bone faerie, you have to go through, it's the only way."

This was not proving to be as easy a task as I'd hoped. Was I risking too much to go after this daughter of Wendy? Tiger Lily's words echoed in my mind, *are you really that selfish?* I hated to admit it, even to myself, but when it came to this girl, this descendent of Wendy, I was that selfish. I had an inexplicable desire to see her, to be with her, no matter the cost.

"OK, I'll go in first. Leave a sizable distance between us. If something goes wrong, you all turn back and return without me." I knew they never would, but I felt the need to give them an out on this one. If they were going to follow me in this selfish endeavor, then it would be on their terms.

I walked tentatively into the narrow crevice, turning sideways and sidestepping just to fit through. The rocks felt tight against me, scraping my arms and tearing at my clothing. The wind picked up and howled as it passed through the planes of stone. The hair on my arms stood alert as a shiver ripped down my spine. I could have sworn I heard the cackling of an old woman carried on the wind.

I made it through the rock without issue and found myself in a glade, surrounded by towering trees. Just as it was with the pirates, the barren ground here was also devoid of any life. Only a cold mist clung to the ground as it rolled and swirled across the glade. A small, dilapidated shack made of weathered grey wood sat in the center of the opening, a patchwork of green moss enveloping it. The thatched roof was caving in in some places.

The only signs of life were the small puffs of smoke rising from the chimney. The shack was surrounded by a partition of bones that had been buried into the ground. They were staggered haphazardly around like some sort of fence. More bones hung from strings in the trees, swaying and clattering together even though there was no longer a breeze.

Tripp came out of the fissure first, followed by Ryder and then Eben with Lilleybell perched on his shoulder.

"Lill, go fly over to the house and see if she's in there."

Her brow drew together and she pouted her lips, "Why do I have to go? I brought you here, my job's done."

I plucked her off of Eben's shoulder and held her in front of my face.

"You said you were here to help and you are *my* faerie after all. None of us can get close enough without giving away our position. Besides, she won't want you anyway, your bones wouldn't amount to anything."

Her little body glowed red, she was pissed at me, but she dutifully went on her way and slipped into the house through a crack in the siding. She returned after a moment, shaking her head.

"She's not there, the place is empty."

"I can't imagine she's gone far, she has a fire going," I thought aloud.

"Maybe we got lucky and she's not here. We can breeze in, get what we need and get the hell out of here," Ryder said hopefully.

"I'm thinking that's not likely Ry, but good try," Tripp replied.

"Eben, give me that head you took from the pirate. I'm going to go make an offering. If she is here, I'll try and draw her out and keep her distracted while the rest of you go in and find the skull Tiger Lily's looking for."

Eben handed me the bloodied shirt that contained the head and I started walking toward the house, hands raised.

"Bone faerie... " I bellowed. "I know you're here. I've come to trade with you. Show yourself and see what I have to offer."

It was completely silent as I approached the shack, not even the creatures of the forest made a sound. Reaching the front door, I swiveled my head around to see if I could catch a glimpse of anything.

A raspy voice emerged from the quietness, "It is not often that I receive willing guests. But I knew you would come. You have kept me waiting a long time, Peter Pan." Her words came in a wet hiss. I kept looking around trying to locate where the voice had come from, but it seemed to echo throughout the entire glade, giving nothing away.

"Seems like you know me, why don't you show yourself so we can talk, face to face," I shouted out to the forest beyond.

A sinister chuckle filled the air, "Tell me, why have you come?"

"I thought you knew I was coming."

"Knew you were coming, yes. It is the why of it, that the Divine keeps from me."

"So you can see the future?" The idea of soliciting the future from her was tempting. I could control the course of everything if I knew what was coming next. This could be the perfect distraction while the boys stole the skull. If I played my cards right, I'd come away from this mission with more than just a skull.

"I see you in the bones... see your future," she let out a low sinister laugh. "An oddity to be sure. A human that seduced a realm, an island that stopped the very passage of time for you. How could I resist looking into a future like that."

"Tell me more," I insisted, trying to keep her talking. I couldn't see the boys, but that was a good thing. Hopefully they were getting themselves into position.

"Greedy... selfish... deceiver. You have not answered me. Tell me why you are here and I will give you a crumb."

"I am here on a mission. I need answers. What will be the consequences of the decisions I am making now?"

"You answer a question with a question, and give me nothing. I see the web of lies you spin, but you see, I am the spider and not the gnat."

"I answered your question. I told you why I came, now you owe me a crumb."

"Like your web, everything the Divine creates is connected by strings. It pulls and binds and draws us together upon its whim. The bones speak to me, they tell me you are a crucial string in this realm, in all the realms. Strings are being pulled toward you, but it must be so in the right time."

"The right time, what does that mean? When is the right time?"

"A river is born in a mountain. It is weak and small. To become mighty, it must collect its strings, pull them all together as it journeys to the sea. It cannot bypass the journey, it will not be strong enough to carve a path in the land if it does."

I pulled my fingers through my hair in frustration. Her cryptic words didn't give me anything. She only spoke in riddles that I knew would drive me crazy when I tried to decipher them later.

"You haven't told me anything."

"Ungrateful! You come to my home, spewing questions and then you are not satisfied with the answers. Maybe it is you that is not asking the right questions."

"I have an offering for you." I pulled the severed head from the makeshift bag. I held it up in display as I turned, still not sure where she was hiding.

"I think you missed this one. I figured I'd bring it back to you. You can have it...if you tell me more."

"You try to offer me trash," She scoffed.

"You took the skulls from the rest of the pirates, what is wrong with this one?"

"This is not my trash, it is your trash. You have nothing of value in this bone." I heard a creaking in the trees behind me. I spun around and looked up just in time to see a dark figure jump from a high tree limb. An expanse of membranous wings shot out from her back. A few powerful strokes had her climbing into the air. She moved so fast that I couldn't make out her features. I watched in awe as she dove toward the ground, dropped down behind a stand of boulders and plucked Ryder from the ground. He struggled to get free, but talon like fingers gripped him tight. She flew to me effortlessly, as if Ryder's added weight was nothing to her. I had severely underestimated the strength of this creature. She landed on the ground before me in a whoosh. The wind from her wings rustled the leaves in a whirlwind around me. Black, eyeless sockets stared in my direction from beneath dark, worn robes. Her sickly, grey skin was as wrinkled as her rumpled robes and appeared to hang from the bones of her face. Her crooked nose protruded like a beak, and tufts of wiry grey hair, stuck out sporadically around her face. She resembled a vulture as she tucked her large wings in behind her. She held Ryder by the neck with one long, taloned hand, and held a bone knife to his throat, with the other.

"Now this— this is something of value," She crooned and took a long sniff of his hair. "Yes, his bones would do nicely."

"He's not up for trade," I seethed at her, my body now postured for battle and my dagger, firmly in hand.

"You wanted answers. This is the price I am asking."

"The deals off, give me back my man, unharmed, and we will leave with my questions unanswered."

"You do not know how valuable the knowledge is. You

have set in motion things that must come to fruition, the realms depend on it. Don't you want to know what that is?"

"If it's so important to the realms, then why not just tell me. Why extract a price?"

"The fate of the realms is of no importance to me. The Divine has already shown me the stardust of a new existence. I must simply wait to see how this universe plays out."

"I think I'll take my chances."

"Do you see this," she pulled the cowl of her robes down to reveal her decomposing chest. It was sunken in and the skin was completely gone in places, exposing parts of her rib cage and breast bone. It was like a puzzle of unique bones that didn't appear to be her own. The smell of decay wafted from her and invaded my senses. "This one," she tapped her bone knife against the breast bone. Its ashen color stood out against the other white bones and it was pitted and porous as if it was disintegrating in her chest. "This one I took from a Fae prince over a millennium ago. It was very powerful, but its magic is almost gone. I need a replacement. His will do nicely until I can find a powerful Fae to make a more permanent replacement. *That* is already in the works for a later date." She licked her chapped lips as if the idea made her hungry.

I heard the sickening thud before I saw the hatchet protruding from her chest. She let out a piercing wail and I turned briefly to see Eben returning to his cover behind the shack. When I turned back to the bone faerie, she was sucking in deep, gasping breaths.

"You fools, you cannot kill me. I am the wind, the river, the rain. You can alter my course, but you cannot kill me."

"Pan... " Ryder called to me. "Give the girl a kiss for me. I sure hope she's fucking worth it."

"No!" I yelled at him, but it was too late. He elbowed the Fae in the gut and she relaxed her hold just enough for him to twist toward her and ram his palm into the butt of the hatchet that was still protruding from her breast bone. The force of the blow shattered the bone in her chest and a blinding light radiated out as a force of power exploded from within, lifting me off my feet, sending me sprawling. Her shriek filled my ears, rattling my brain.

I came to a moment later, totally disoriented and my head pounded in my skull. What the hell had just happened? When the fog in my mind cleared I saw the bone faerie, laid out on the ground in a heap of robes, not moving, and Ryder lay beside her. I scrambled on my hands and knees to him, not sure I could trust my legs to hold me up just yet. Grabbing his shoulder I rolled his limp body onto his back. Tripp and Eben ran up beside me.

"Lill! Where the fuck is Lill!"

"I'm here Peter, I'm here!"

"Is he—" I couldn't finish the sentence. I wouldn't, because he couldn't be dead. I wouldn't allow it. Without answering me, Lill flew over him, releasing a cascade of faerie dust over his body. I breathed a sigh of relief as it began pooling together, like mercury, and centered over his heart. Had he been dead, it would have slid off of him like droplets of water.

"Press here on the dust. You need to restart his heart," Lill commanded.

I did as she asked and placed my palms over the faerie dust on his chest and pressed down hard. His whole body convulsed. I could feel the shock of the faerie dust running through my hands and up my shoulders. He drew a large gasp of air and then settled back on the ground, still unconscious.

"He should be alright for now, but we need to get him to a healer. I can't say for sure what that bitch's magic has done to him internally."

"What about the bone faerie, is she dead?" Eben asked as he peered over at her limp body.

"She cannot die," Lill answered. "When Ryder destroyed her breast bone, he put her in a sort of hibernation. Until someone makes her whole again and replaces that bone, she's trapped inside that body."

"Well what should we do with her? We can't take her back with us, but who knows what could happen if the wrong people make her whole again," Tripp said.

"We have to get Ryder out of here as soon as possible and it will take all of us to fly him out. Let's bury her under some rocks and we can make a plan for her later. You guys put together something we can carry Ryder out on. I've gotta get that skull for Tiger Lily, or else this whole fucking trip was in vain."

Eben glared at me. He would never forgive me for what just happened, especially if Ryder didn't pull through. I couldn't dwell on that now, so I bolted into the old shack to find my prize.

The place was filthy and every wall was stacked with bones. The hollowed eyes of thousands of skulls stared at me, sending chills up my spine. I pulled a small drawing that Tiger Lily had given me, with a rendering of the skull she was looking for. It was that of a small antlered predator, with long curving canines and large eye sockets. I frantically scanned the room, I was anxious to get what I needed and get back to Ryder. Most of the bones were human, apparently we humans were an easy target.

"Where the fuck are you?" I mumbled to myself. I turned over the scant furniture in the room, but came up with nothing. There was no place to hide an object of value in this simple house. *If it were me, where would I hide my most prized possession?* The image of Wendy's thimble came to mind and I absently reached to my belt, knowing it was securely tucked into a pouch there.

I ran out of the house and went to search the lifeless body of the bone faerie. Pilfering through her robes, I found a pouch tucked into the inner lining. I pulled it out and opened the suede sack to reveal the skull. It was about the size of my hand. It was fox like, only with small antlers. Definitely not from any creature I had ever seen. Geometric patterns were etched into the bone. I couldn't fathom why this small skull was of such value to Tiger Lily. I would have to do some more digging. If I was going to hand this over, then I would need to know what it was capable of.

"Find it?" Tripp asked.

"Yep," I sighed. "Now let's get the fuck out of here."

Chapter Eight
A STORY FOR ANOTHER DAY

Y ou have it then?" Tiger Lily asked, her eyes wide with expectation.

"Of course I have it."

"Oh Peter... " she laughed incredulously, as if she wasn't fully convinced that I wouldn't die on that mission. "I knew you were the right person to collect it for me."

"You sent us in there to be slaughtered. Did you hear what happened to Ryder? He's still hasn't come to yet," I barked at her.

"I heard that the best healers in the village have tended to him and he will be just fine. You are getting a bit too carried away, don't you think."

"You didn't tell me everything."

"I told you what you needed to know to bring the artifact back to me. But I am curious, how were you able to get it from her?"

"That's a story for another day, just know her body lies dormant under a cairn."

"Excellent. Now we don't have to worry about her coming to retrieve it. I must say, I am impressed, Peter."

"Tell me what it can do," I insisted.

"I told you, it contains old magic that I can use to keep us all safe. *If* it comes to that."

"You're being deceptively vague."

"Magic is something your realm is not blessed with, so it is something that you are just unable to comprehend. Please, Peter trust me on this one, you're putting it in the right hands." She held out her palm, expecting me to hand it over, no further explanation needed.

"Peter," she said, exasperated as I didn't move to give her the skull. "I don't think you are in any position to deny me my part of our bargain. If you'd rather I take all that I know about this daughter of Wendy, to the Council, I will. I can recommend that it's best we end the entire Darling line to keep the secrets of Neverland safe. I only have to give the command to my sentries and it would be over, your little obsession would no longer be an issue."

"You wouldn't dare," I growled.

"Give me the skull Peter and I will happily turn a blind eye to whatever it is you want with this human girl."

I huffed in irritation and pulled the skull from my belt placing it, reluctantly in her outstretched hand.

"See, I knew we could come to an understanding. I am your friend. Once you get this Wendy girl out of your system, I think it's time we explore just how strong we could be together."

"Tiger Lily, I'm not—"

"Shhh, let's not discuss this now. You know, as well as I do, that I am your best match. Neverland brought you to me so that we could rule together, arm in arm. The children we bear will inherit the universe."

"That's just a bit ambitious, don't you think?"

"With the two of us together, anything is possible. Sooner or later you will figure that out. But for now, go and enjoy your *tryst* with this girl and know that when it's all over, you *will* return to me and fulfill your destiny."

This isn't the End

OH NO, this is just the beginning. Second to the Right Volume I of the Neverland Chronicles, is available now on Amazon. Continue on for a special sneak peek at Second to the Right.

THE STORY CONTINUES...
SECOND TO THE RIGHT THE NEVERLAND CHRONICLES VOL I

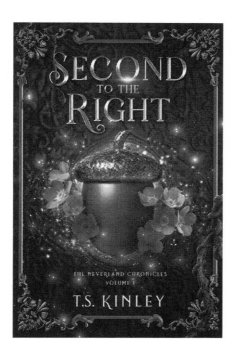

Gwendolyn Mary Darling Carlisle's young life has been a saga of misfortune. After a tragic accident unexpectedly took her parents, Gwen finds herself the sole caregiver for her ailing sister. It's her eighteenth birthday. With responsibilities weighing heavy, she struggles to find something worth celebrating. Everything in her life has fallen apart. That is, until she finds a mysterious man in her bedroom.

Peter Pan has returned to the Darling estate. Only the boy from Neverland, who refused to grow up, has in fact grown into an alluring man. It's time for spring cleaning and he's determined to bring a descendant of Wendy back to Neverland with him.

Gwen is swept off her feet and across the Veil. Engulfed in a fantastical world of mermaids, Fae, and Peter's new band of Lost Boys. As she gives herself over to the wonder of Neverland and the affections of Peter and his Lost Boys, she finds herself living out hedonistic fantasies that she could have only ever dreamed about. But not everything is as it seems in Neverland. Her memories of home, and her beloved sister are fading. A treasured family heirloom, a locket with its own ties to Neverland, is the only tether of the sister she'd left behind and the life she is obligated to return to. The fairytales she'd heard as a child only hinted at the truth. Neverland bears some dark secrets. Confronted with deception and lies, Gwen must decide who and what to believe.

Available on Amazon now

Continue on for a sneak peek inside

SECOND TO THE RIGHT SNEAK PEEK
PROLOGUE -PETER

It would be different this time. I felt it in my bones.

The past few days of watching her had made that abundantly clear. When I'd returned through the Veil from Neverland, it felt as though no time had passed. Although time is funny like that, how it quietly sneaks past you. But as I sat, yet again, and watched through the window, from the outside looking in, it was obvious that everything had changed.

This time, I'd perched myself in the large oak in the backyard, which was perfectly positioned for me to see into her window. The home was the familiar old Victorian, but nothing else was the same. The gas lamps had been replaced, and the lights were much brighter than before. The furniture, the music and the girl, were all different. It had been an interesting few days as I'd watched, biding my time before I approached her. I ventured close enough at times to listen to her, waiting to see if she would tell the same stories as Wendy, but she told no stories.

She was a curious creature. I couldn't keep myself from watching her, puzzling over what she was doing and what she was saying.

Tonight, she had sat and stared at her reflection for hours, playing with her hair and putting on makeup. The outfit she had on complimented her figure in a way that had me staring at her lasciviously. Her long legs were outlined in black and the soft brown of her hair fell in waves around her face. The gentle swell of her breasts in that revealing shirt kept drawing my attention.

The way she looked had my heart racing as it does in the heat of battle and I felt a sudden urge to touch her. I broke my stare, trying to get my wayward thoughts under control as I raked my fingers through my unruly hair.

This was an entirely different experience than the last time I'd been here. This was no girl that I was watching, she was definitely a woman. I was different as well. My boyish youth, that I had clung to for so long had slowly leached away. The universe had different plans for the boy who refused to grow up. I had been forced to come to terms with the fact that absolutely nothing was permanent, no matter how much you rebelled against it. It seemed I was doomed to learn that lesson over and over again.

I wanted so badly to breeze through her window, proclaiming myself as the notorious Peter Pan and spend the night basking in her smiles as I regaled her with stories of pirates and mermaids. I got as far as springing the latch, before I thought better of it and pulled away, worried that I might scare her.

I flattened myself against the outside wall as she came to close the window. She paused there and made no move to leave. I was closer to her than I had ever been before and she was intoxicating. I could smell her, fresh and sweet, like ripe berries in summer. Her skin was creamy and smooth, her lips pouty, full and parted. She was a vision in the moonlight.

She moved away from the window as her sister called out for her. Sadly, I had noticed that her sister's health was waning, and she did not have much time left in this world. It was a shame that she had such a fleeting spirit. But this girl, this sister, was vibrant, and full of life and something altogether different.

I reached into my belt and pulled Wendy's "kiss" from the leather pouch attached there. I rolled the cool metal dome in my fingers and remembered our time together. I had been naive back then. I hadn't realized at the time, but Wendy had been a key catalyst in my life. She had changed me so completely, for both the good, and the bad. Would this girl leave her mark on me as well? Did I even want to put myself through that again? It almost broke me last time. But, the more I watched her, the more I convinced myself, that if I could only get her to come back with me, I didn't need to have all the answers right then. I had time. Against my better judgment, I was determined to bring her back with me. While she explored Neverland, I could explore her.

I was brought back to reality as I realized the two sisters were leaving the house. This was different than her normal routine that I had become accustomed to. I felt a twinge of annoyance that she would leave and deprive me of watching her. With a huff of impatience, I settled into the oak tree to wait for her to return.

I wished, briefly, that I had brought Lilleybell along to keep me company, but faeries had no room for more than one emotion at a time. Her jealousy could be all consuming and I didn't want to make the same mistakes I had made with Wendy. Alone with my thoughts, I began to get nervous, which was a relatively foreign feeling for me. If she decided not to go with me, would I stay here with her? Could I resign from my responsibilities back in Neverland? I had a vision of myself picking her up, throwing her over my shoulder, and taking her against her will to Neverland. Alas, that was something only a bastard pirate would do, those uncivilized fucks, and I wouldn't lower myself to their level.

I wondered what she would think about the Lost Boys? They had been keen to hear about the girl that I'd planned to bring back. Would they have the same feelings toward her as I did? I felt a flash of senseless jealousy at the idea of her with them. This girl was making my rational thinking go out the window.

I began to get restless just after midnight. I'm not the type to wait around for anything. I had grown tired of my tormenting thoughts, and I was spiraling down a rabbit hole of negativity. I decided it was best that I return home. Just as I was about to take my leave, and head second to the right, she returned home. I perked up instantly, thrilled at my luck. She had arrived just in time so I could continue my appreciation of her.

As they made their way into the house, I could tell something was off. Her sister was fawning over my girl, wrapping a supportive arm around her as they made their way inside. I'm not entirely sure why I thought of her as 'my girl'. I had never really considered Wendy or any one of her daughters as mine before, but my mind grabbed a hold of the notion and it just felt right with her.

The overall mood of the pair was sad and solemn. I wondered what had changed from the cheery mood they had been in when they'd left. Yet more questions surrounding this girl. She had my mind in overdrive thinking about what might've happened. I watched intently, hoping she would return to her room. The minutes ticked by like hours as I waited for her to appear.

She finally entered her room and walked dejectedly to the small bathroom and closed the door. I decided to get close, placing my ear to the window to see if I might hear anything that would clue me into her stark change in mood. My concern for her felt like a knot of tension in my chest and the need to make sure she was ok took over.

I could hear the sound of the shower, pouring down in her bathroom for some time. I was torn on what my next move should be. Go in to check on her or continue my wait and watch approach? My indecision was infuriating! She emerged from the bathroom in a cloud of steam. She was wearing low slung, gray sweatpants that gripped low on her hips and a short black top that exposed her flat stomach. Her skin was dewy from the steam in the air and her hair was dripping, leaving wet patches on her shirt, clinging to her chest and showing off her erect nipples.

I sucked in a deep breath as I took her in. I could no longer deny that I wanted her, to mark her and claim her as my own. A dark shadow loomed in the recesses of my mind, what consequences would I face if I followed that path? But one look at her face and my inhibitions left me. I knew that she had been crying. Her makeup was smeared, and her eyes were red and puffy. Why was she crying? The not knowing was driving me crazy.

She sat quietly at her vanity, a blank stare on her face. I looked at her reflection in the mirror, my gaze settled on her soft, caramel eyes and felt a strong desire to protect her, to take her tears away. What was going on with me? I had never felt this carnal and protective before. I was pulled from my thoughts when she swept her arm violently across the vanity, sending bottles crashing to the floor, then promptly sunk her face into her pillowed arms and started crying.

Her raw emotions spurred me into action, all my earlier hesitations forgotten. I sprung the latch in one swift flick of the wrist and landed silently on the floor behind her.

"Girl...why are you crying?"

Wendy's first words to me echoing in my head.

SECOND TO THE RIGHT
CHAPTER 1
THE OPEN WOUND OF BETRAYAL -GWEN

The window was open.

Not everyone can pinpoint the moment their universe was forever altered and relate it to such a mundane thing as opening a window. But that is exactly where my life changed course, and I would never be the same.

It was the cold night air, blustering into the room that drew my attention. The engulfing chill sent an involuntary shiver up my spine. My bedroom curtains billowed in the wind that gusted through the open bay window.

How did that get open? I wondered.

I grasped my shoulders and absently rubbed my arms for warmth. The rusted hardware must have finally given out on the old window, or at least that's what I told myself. My family had owned this house since the 18th century and the logical conclusion was that it was always in some state of disrepair. I sat briefly on the window seat and paused before closing the window. It was a bitter London evening as the last vestiges of winter gave its final breath before relenting to spring. The moon was full tonight, setting a warm glow to the landscape below while the stars peppered the sky above. I smiled and took a moment to enjoy the beauty of it.

The old house groaned in protest with the wind, creating an ethereal moaning as it passed through. I felt the hairs raise on my arms and goose pimples spread across my skin. An odd sense of foreboding crept into me as the crisp air filled my lungs. It was a feeling I couldn't quite discern, something like anticipation mixed with anxiety. I felt an expectation that something was about to happen and it had me on edge.

"Gwen?" my sister, Michaela, called to me from down stairs. "Are you ready yet, birthday girl?"

Disrupting me from my reverie, I quickly pulled the window closed and managed to secure the latch, which was oddly perfect and did nothing to relieve the uneasiness I felt.

"Coming! Just need to grab my purse," I shouted down to her.

I took one final look in the tall mirror before I headed downstairs for our night on the town. I turned to check out how good my ass looked in these leather pants. It was definitely something I would never have picked out on my own, but Michaela had been right about the outfit, even though I would never admit it to her.

The fabric of my blouse clung to me in all the right places, showing off what little cleavage I could manage and the black lace of my bralette peeked out from the deep V neck of the top. Satisfied with my look, I flopped down on my bed, slipping on my favorite peep toe heels and grabbed my purse.

I found Michaela sitting at the kitchen island, staring at the little compact she was holding, intently applying her lipstick. Her face, that had once been so much like mine, now appeared thin and gaunt. Her recent treatments had taken their toll on her. Her beautiful hair had not grown back yet and tonight she sported a sleek, platinum blonde wig with a heavy bang. As children, we had often been confused for twins, but now the stark contrast between us broke my heart.

"Damn, eighteen is looking great on you!" my sister squealed as she noticed me and pulled me into a quick hug. "I wish mum and dad could be here to see you," she added softly, her eyes taking on a far away look as she remembered our late parents.

"Thanks, love," I said, a bit distantly. I was still trying to shake off the feeling I'd had at the window seat and I didn't want to add to it with thoughts of another birthday without my mum and dad.

"Everything okay?" she asked, brows instantly furrowed in concern.

"It's nothing, the bay window blew open and I guess it just creeped me out."

"It's Gram's fault for always filling our heads with her so-called fairytales about this place when we were little."

"Ugh, yes! I remember spending nights awake, petrified that someone was looking in my window because of those stories." She giggled at me as I rolled my eyes and quickly changed topics.

"Are you sure you're up for this tonight?" I asked quietly. I was hoping not to offend her but I was genuinely concerned over what a night of drinking and dancing might do to her frail health.

"Sweetie, I wouldn't miss this for the world! It's not like you turn 18 every day. It's been far too long since we've been able to act our age. So I'm taking you out and we are going to have the night of our lives." Her exuberant voice belied her weakened body.

I decided to put my worries to bed as best I could, because I selfishly wanted to spend this night with her. Not only was it my birthday, but she had just recently finished chemo and her cancer was now in remission for the second time and it was a victory worth celebrating.

"Let me text Jamie that we're leaving and he can meet us at the club."

"Are you sure you want him to come along? You're not going to have as much fun if he's there," she groaned exaggeratedly.

I gave her a chastising look, "Oh stop, can you please just give him a chance? I really like this one Mic."

"I just..." she paused, carefully considering her words. "I just think you can do better. I know you've been swooning over this guy for months now, but I don't trust him. That whole thing with his ex-girlfriend really rubbed me the wrong way."

"He explained that already, Mic! Nothing happened, she just needed closure and I think it was sweet of him not to blow her off. He told me it's over and I believe him," I rebutted in his defense. She was never going to let that go.

"My gut is telling me that something is off with him. But I've said my piece and if you trust him, then that will have to be good enough for me." Her words sounded genuinely concerned. "I can only hope, when you go away to university this fall, you'll meet some smoldering book nerd in one of your literature classes, who will make you forget all about Jamie Holder."

But Jamie Holder wasn't just some random boy. He had been the object of my affection since grade school. Albeit my affections had always been from afar, but all that had changed when he had finally noticed me in our last semester at school. I could agree that he wasn't perfect, but neither was I and I rationalized it by admitting that I couldn't hold him to impossible standards. Plus, the fact that he was hot as hell definitely hindered my better judgment when it came to him.

"Well, your intuition is wrong this time. I actually think I'm starting to fall in love with him," I admitted hesitantly, putting hopeful words into the infatuation I'd been feeling. I almost laughed at the look of shock on her face.

"Okay, this conversation is getting way too deep and it's your birthday so I'm not gonna argue with you about your lousy choice in men. We'll table this one until tomorrow."

I smiled at her and brushed it off, she had never liked any of the men I dated. She was like the boy who cried wolf. This time I wasn't about to listen to her warnings, especially not when my tall, dark and handsome crush had finally taken an interest in me. But she was right about one thing, I didn't want to argue. It was my eighteenth birthday after all.

The club was packed with half dressed people, the air thick and filled with the smell of musky sweat and stale beer. Michaela pulled me toward the VIP section at the back of the club where she had a quick exchange with the large bouncer standing guard. He pulled aside the velvet ropes and ushered us in. The swanky lounge area was filled with beautiful people on sleek white, modern couches, flirting and drinking around marble coffee tables. I spotted Jamie, staring down at his phone while he waited for me in an area marked as reserved.

"Hey babe!" he called when he saw me walk up, quickly pocketing his phone. I smiled a stupid school girl smile at him and bit my lip.

"Hey!" I said as I reached up on my tiptoes to give him a kiss. I was planning on a quick peck, but he deepened it and thrust his tongue into my mouth, tasting me briefly before pulling back and leaving me dazed.

"You are killing me in those pants. Turn around and let me see that ass."

"Nice Jamie, could've maybe started with Happy Birthday?" Michaela scoffed, her tone dripping with disapproval.

"Nice to see you too, Mickey," he responded tersely, not even bothering to look over at her, which was a good thing because she was staring daggers at him. She hated being called Mickey and he knew it. Her glare was interrupted by the sound of his phone chiming in his pocket with a new text.

"You gonna get that?" Mic asked flippantly, still holding onto her grudge. He continued to ignore her and turned to me.

"I'm putting my phone on silent so nothing can interrupt us tonight. Come on, let me buy you your first drink."

He placed his hand on the small of my back, ushering me toward the bar. Once I was in front of him, I heard a resounding *crack*, accompanied by a sharp sting on my ass as he spanked me, hard. I blushed uncontrollably. Michaela must have been mortified, but he made me feel sexy, even if it was a bit crude.

"Plenty more spankings for my birthday girl tonight," he whispered into my ear, his deep, husky voice full of innuendo.

He easily pushed through to the bar, his six foot five frame towering over almost every one. He got quick service as the female bartender catered to him right away, her voice high and flirty, her eyes lingering over him too long for my liking. He gave her a charming smile as he turned back to me with our drinks. He handed me over a shot of Jäger.

I hate Jäger.

I felt a moment of aggravation that he hadn't asked me what I wanted, but in typical girl fashion, I convince myself that it was sweet of him to get my drink.

"Thank you!" I yell to him, the loud techno drowning out our voices.

"Alright babe, down the hatch and let me get you on that dance floor." He pounded the shot and looked at me expectantly.

Like a child anticipating Gram's cough syrup, I held my breath and managed to get the nasty liquid down in one gulp. I had to continue to hold my breath to keep the drink down as my stomach rebelled. Michaela was instantly beside me, pushing a Captain and Coke into my hands. I gave her a relieved look. I took a few quick sips and finally got the taste of the Jäger out of my mouth. Jamie downed a second shot and grabbed my hand, pulling me to the dance floor.

The bass from the club pulsed through me as we danced. I was slicked in sweat, with strands of my hair plastered to my chest. I let my body sway to the music, intermittently sipping at my drink. My hand was wet and sticky as it kept spilling, but I didn't care. My glass hadn't been empty all night. I think Michaela was set on getting me sloppy drunk tonight. I was thankful that my shift at the cafe tomorrow didn't start until late in the afternoon. I had a feeling that my hangover would be brutal. I pushed the thought from my mind, I just wanted to act my age for once and not worry about my responsibilities for one night. I knew more alcohol would help with that. My inhibitions vanished with each passing drink and I began to shamelessly grind my ass against Jamie. He kept pace with me, grabbing my hips and pulling me closer.

"You are so sexy," he growled in my ear. "You have to come home with me tonight."

I giggled, peeking over my shoulder at him, giving him my best attempt at a seductive smile. I had promised to spend the night with Michaela, but I was enjoying his attention so much that I couldn't bring myself to turn him down just yet. Michaela appeared in front of me and grabbed my hand, attempting to pull me from Jamie. I was about to protest at her intrusion and being a total buzzkill to my libido when she leaned in to whisper in my ear, "I have something I need to give you. Can you please come with me?" She was insistent and continued her attempt to pull me from the dance floor. I turned back to Jamie with an apologetic look.

"I'll be right back, I promise. Mic just needs me for a minute." He shook his head at me, looking irritated at the interruption.

"Yeah, sure, whatever." His tone conveyed his irritation.

My older sister had always been overprotective when it came to boys. It was frustrating at times, but I couldn't fault her for it. I knew it came from a place of love and any boy worth his weight would understand that. I just desperately hoped that Jamie would. She pulled me to the couch that she'd reserved for us in the VIP lounge and I sat down hard. My head was spinning from all the alcohol and my gracefulness had gone out the window.

"Happy birthday baby sis," she crooned sweetly as she handed me a small box wrapped in golden paper and topped with a red bow.

I looked at her with that 'you shouldn't have' look and pulled her in for a hug before I even opened the tiny box. I pulled off the wrapping paper and opened the gift to find a familiar piece of jewelry nestled inside. I lifted out the gilded acorn locket that had been my mother's, and her mother's before that, and on and on, for more than a hundred years.

I popped the delicate clasp and looked for the inscription that I knew was inside, 'To die will be an awfully big adventure.' The quote had always seemed morbid to me and it gave me chills reading it now. I never understood why anyone would put such a quote on a prized piece of jewelry.

The heirloom locket now also included a miniature photo of Michaela and I, smiling and happy during a time before my parent's accident and her cancer had cast a gloom over everything. The words and the image affected me in my altered state so much that I felt the prick of tears come to my eyes. The drinks were making me overly sentimental.

"The quote was meant for both of us, Gwen. It's as much about living, as it is about death. Momento mori," she stated, answering the question I hadn't spoken allowed.

I stared at her in shocked awe. Her use of the Latin phrase meaning "Remember that you must die" was so profound. For the first time, the rationale for the inscription made sense to me. It was a reminder to live your life in the moment, with the knowledge that you will eventually die.

"I'm going to be okay. We both have big adventures awaiting us, just down different paths."

"I don't understand, why are you giving this to me? Mum left it to you. You're the oldest, that's how it works," I croaked out in a shaky voice, unable to say anything more or else I would break out in real tears. But I knew why she was giving it to me. I just refused to put that thought into words, but she did it for me instead.

"Gwen," she said my name gently, "this locket is meant to be handed down and I won't be here long enough to make that happen. It has to go to you. Here, let me put it on for you."

"How can you say that? You just reached remission. It's not coming back this time! I don't want the locket, it's yours." My emotional mind rationalized that if I just didn't accept it, then the tragic future she was painting wouldn't come true.

"Gwendolyn Mary Darling Carlisle, you know the odds are slim to none that the remission will last. This last treatment only bought us a little more time. So you *will* accept it because it is mine to give and I am giving it to you now. I want to give it of my own free will rather than you putting it in a box with the rest of my things when I'm gone." Her stern voice left little room for me to argue.

"If I accept it, it's not because I think you are going anywhere, and you have to agree to take it back when you have a daughter of your own to give it to."

She looked at me with pity in her eyes, pity of all things. I should be pitying her, she was the one casually talking about her early death as if it was no big deal.

"Okay, Gwen," she conceded, obviously not wanting to upset me any further. "Now turn around and let me put it on you."

I swept my sweat soaked hair to one side. Cold air ominously rushed down my exposed neck, chilling me instantly. I turned my back to her quickly, hoping she wouldn't see the fear in my eyes. The fear of what she was trying to tell me, by giving me this locket. She clasped the pendant in place and it settled beautifully between my breasts. I grasped it and the weight of it felt oddly warm and comforting in my hand.

"It looks beautiful on you, just like it did on mum," she said appraisingly. A proud smile lit up her face as she looked me over. Even her eyes seemed glassy for a brief moment before she was on her feet again and pulling me back to the bar.

"Time for another drink!" she exclaimed and weaseled her way to the front of the bar and ordered us another round.

"A toast!" she yelled as she handed me a shot of Johnnie Walker. Oh she knew me so well. "To my baby sister! Cheers to good health and a man who is sexy as fuck and will fulfill your wildest dreams!"

"Cheers!" we both yelled in unison, clinking our shot glasses together and throwing them back. I turned back to the dance floor and attempted to pull Mic with me but she pulled back.

"Go on without me, I'm gonna sit at the bar and people watch. Go find Jamie and enjoy yourself." She gave me a one-sided smile as if she could only be partially happy for me when it came to Jamie. I smiled back at her and headed off on my own to find him.

I danced my way through the packed floor, not seeing him anywhere. I'd started getting nervous, worried he was avoiding me. I desperately hoped he wouldn't be too pissed at me over Mic's mother hen routine. I was about to head to the restrooms to see if I could find him there, when a white dress caught my attention. I could make out the back of a curvy blonde in a shadowed corner of the night club. The black lights caused her dress to glow purple in the darkness. Her hair was cascading down the back of her skin tight dress and I could see that she wasn't alone.

A man's hand was cupping her ass. When she turned her head to the side, I was instantly frozen in place when I saw that the man groping her was Jamie! He pulled her hips into his like he'd just done to me on the dance floor, all the while he kissed up her neck and took her mouth. I stared in shock, completely stunned, my heart dropping at the sight of them together. I watched as the two of them made out in front of me, allowing it to go on much longer than I should. Before I knew what I was doing, I marched over to them, feeling utterly enraged, and yanked at the hand that he was still cupping her ass with.

"Jamie Fucking Holder!" I knew I was feeling more bold than usual. Normally, I would have just turned around and ran from the entire situation.

At my intrusion, the blonde turned toward me and

recognition hit me. I was stuck in a moment of complete disbelief. Of course it was Bella! The girl Jamie had been dating before me. The girl he'd sworn that he no longer had any feelings for.

"Gwen, it's not... it's not what you think. Bella and I were just... talking," he stumbled over his words as he stepped toward me, his inebriated mind trying to play catch up to the situation.

"I think I know what I saw!" I shouted back at him, I could feel the disbelief dissolve and give way to anger again. I struggled to keep my temper as Bella gave me a malicious smile from her position behind him. He tried to grab my hand but I yanked it back quickly, the idea of him touching me now turning my stomach.

"Can we talk 'bout this later? You're drunk... I'm drunk... you're not thinking clearly." He tried to make me question myself and the irrational girl who was still holding onto hope was tempted to believe him. But, Bella destroyed all of my contemplating.

She stepped from behind him, pressed her chest against him and said, "I'll let you handle this with your little friend, Jamie. Text me once you've cleared things up." She planted a slow and sultry kiss on his cheek, leaving her mark of red lipstick behind. He did nothing to stop her or push her away. She sauntered off into the crowd, completely indifferent, as if she hadn't just dropped a bomb on my relationship.

"Is that who you were texting earlier?" I was fuming as I

remembered him on his phone when we first arrived. I grabbed at his pocket in a flash and pulled his phone out before he had a chance to react, the alcohol making him slow.

"Gwen don't touch my... you're acting like a fucking child!" He tried to belittle me, but I needed to know the truth. The screen sprung to life, illuminating my face in the dark club, and there were the unread texts from Bella.

Hurry up and ditch her.
Take me home already! I'm not going to wait 4ever for you 2 end things with her.

Realization hit me that I had been his side piece. That he had been sleeping with me while still carrying on a relationship with her. Our relationship was a foregone conclusion and he was simply waiting for the opportune time to dump me. Clearly my birthday was it. I thought I was going to be sick right there on the dance floor.

My fight or flight response began to kick in at this point and I chose the latter. I couldn't stand to look at him. I turned to leave, but Jamie grabbed my wrist and held me in place.

"Don't walk away from me," his words slightly slurred. I tried to pull away from him but he only tightened his grip, pain shooting up my arm.

"Stop it Jamie! You're hurting me! Let me go!" I screamed at him as I continued to struggle against his iron grip.

"Nope... not letting you go." He chuckled in my face, the smell of alcohol hot on his breath. "You're coming home with me and we're gonna... we're gonna work this out. You've been shaking your ass at me all night. I know that's what you really want. Don't be a tease and let's get out of here."

I stared at him in disgust. Was it the drinks talking, or had he always been a total dick? Had I been blind to it all this time? I began to feel panicked now, his tight grip was unrelenting and the pain only intensified the more I struggled. I needed to get away, now, but he was so much bigger than me. My mind was sluggish and there was only one thing I could think to do.

I stepped toward him as if I was giving in. He smirked at me, but the moment I got close, I kneed him in the crotch with as much force as I could muster. He grunted and doubled over in pain, releasing my wrist. I took advantage and fled through the crowd. I could hear him calling out my name behind me. My smaller frame allowed me to make my way through the throng of people and I lost him quickly as I made my way to the exit. I held it together until I burst through the doors and then the tears began to flow.

I wasn't thinking clearly. I just kept seeing the two of them together on repeat in my brain. Michaela had been right not to trust him all along. I needed to find Michaela, and we needed to leave before Jamie could find me. Mic would know what to say to calm me down, even if I knew she would be silently thinking *told you so* the whole time. I knew she wouldn't throw it in my face, at least not for a while anyway. I just wanted to go home, put on some frumpy pajamas and hibernate under my blankets until I couldn't cry anymore. I pulled my phone out of my purse and texted Mic.

I need you now, meet me outside.

Within moments, Michaela busted through the doors of the club looking wide eyed and frantic.

"What happened?" Her voice was full of empathy as she took me in her arms. I'd been constantly wiping the tears from my face with the back of my hand. I must have looked like an absolute mess with black mascara smeared across my face.

"You were right, and I don't want to talk about it. Can you please take me home?" The statement started off strong but quickly fizzled out into a sob.

"Oh Sweetie, I'm so sorry." She pulled me in for a hug, but I didn't feel like hugging, I just felt heavy. She hugged me anyway, patting the back of my hair as if I was a child. She pulled away and looked me over, landing on my wrist and gently holding it up to inspect the bruises that had already started to form there.

"Did he do this to you?" she asked, her voice coming out cold and harsh, in a way I'd never heard before.

"It's nothing. Let's just go before he finds us," I deflected.

"I'm going to kick his fucking ass!" I gave an involuntary chuckle at the preposterous idea, but she was dead serious. The open wound of the betrayal was still so fresh, that the laugh seemed inappropriate and it was gone in an instant.

"Please Mic, I just want to go home."

SECOND TO THE RIGHT
THE NEVERLAND CHRONICLES VOL I

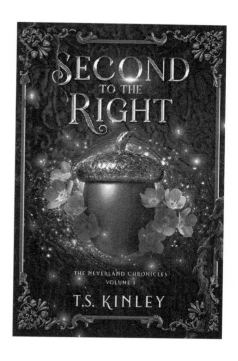

www.TSKinleyBooks.com

Available on Amazon

Be sure to subscribe to our newsletter for the latest news and updates. You'll receive a bonus chapter from Second to the Right in your welcome email.

STRAIGHT ON TILL MORNING
THE NEVERLAND CHRONICLES VOL II

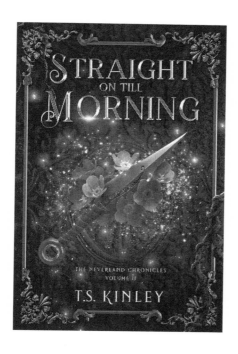

www.TSKinleyBooks.com

Available on Amazon

Be sure to subscribe to our newsletter for the latest news and updates.

QUEEN OF THE LOST BOYS
THE NEVERLAND CHRONICLES VOL III

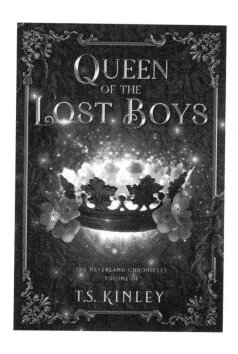

www.TSKinleyBooks.com

Available on Amazon

Be sure to subscribe to our newsletter for the latest news and updates.

Also Available

The Smut Diaries

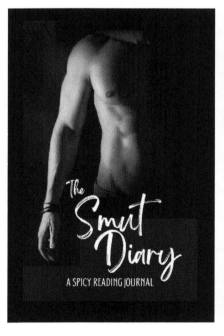

THE SMUT DIARY IS A READING JOURNAL FOR THOSE WHO LIKE IT SPICY. A QUINTESSENTIAL "BLACK BOOK" TO TRACK ALL YOUR BOOK BOYFRIEND AFFAIRS.

ABOUT THE AUTHOR

T. S. Kinley is a passion project created by two sisters with a shared obsession and vision. We came together with the dream of creating something beautiful, imaginative, and yes... SEXY. *Once Upon a Time...* it all began with sisterly gossip about erotica and romance novels. Our conversations quickly became fantasies about our own desires to author such work. We would muse how some day in a utopian future, our fantasy would become reality. Ultimately we decided rather than wait for the future to find us, we would create utopia ourselves. Using our love of books, natural gift of creativity, and some savvy study on publishing itself, the concept for our very first book was born. We started off as a Cosmetologist and an RN, and quickly developed into a dynamic writing team with a style that lends a unique perspective to our books.

If you haven't signed up already, please subscribe to the T.S. Kinley Newsletter.

Receive exclusive sneak peeks on new releases, contests and other spicy content.

Visit www.TSKinleyBooks.com and sign up today!

Follow T.S. Kinley on social media. Let's be friends! Check out our Instagram, Facebook, Pinterest, and Tic Tok pages and get insights into the beautifully, complicated mind of not one, but two authors! You have questions, something you are dying to know about the amazing characters we've created? Join us online, we love to engage with our readers!

AUTHOR

Made in the USA
Las Vegas, NV
25 November 2023